The 34th Year

A Horror Novel-The Lifestyle Detox Series

By Shynita Phillips Abu

Dedication

This book is lovingly dedicated to my late mother,

Theresa Phillips-Goode, whose strength, wisdom, and

prayers live on through me.

To my children, who are my reason to fight, write, and

believe in Do-Overs.

And above all, to God—my refuge, my fortress, my

Deliverer—for carrying me through the Flood and

proving that love conquers darkness.

Acknowledgments

I give all glory to God, who gave me vision and breath to write this testimony in horror form. Thank you to every sister and brother who has supported the Empower Me Network, believed in the Lifestyle Detox, and carried this message forward. This book exists because survival turned into purpose, and purpose turned into legacy.

Prologue

The Law of the Thirty-Fourth Year

Every 34 years, the Abyssal Flood rises, Azraghul awakens, and the systems of man collapse. Children are shielded until 12; beyond that, each soul is weighed.

Reflection & Exhortation

⚖️ Who would you be if your titles, jobs, and systems vanished?

🎇 **Action Prompt:** Write down what you would want Luminar to find in your soul.

Table of Contents

Chapter 1 – Summary

At age 34, I had quit weed and pornography after years of bondage. My Nigerian husband, whom I had sponsored, mocked my prayers and provoked me. When the Abyssal Flood rose, Azraghul devoured him brutally and dragged his soul into the flood. But Luminar spared me, commissioning me to write, empower, and begin the Empower Me Network.

Reflection & Exhortation

1. What chains must you lay down today?

2. What patterns of abuse or stagnation have you tolerated?

❄ Action Prompt: Write one toxic pattern you will not carry into tomorrow.

Chapter 1

The First Testimony (Family)

I was twelve years old when the first chain wrapped around me — pornography. At nineteen, another link tightened — weed. From twelve until thirty-four, I lived shackled to both. Porn by night. Weed by day. And a toxic marriage on top of it all.

He was a Nigerian man. I had brought him over, sponsored him, believing we had true love, a divine connection. I thought God Himself had written our story. I sacrificed, I invested, I trusted.

But little did I know — he was using me for his own gain.

And still, I stayed. Because I took my vows seriously. Til death do us part wasn't just words to me. It was my covenant with God.

So I endured.

Even when he mocked my prayers.

Even when he provoked me until I was jailed for fighting back.

Even when he Face Timed other women while I bled from childbirth.

I stayed, because I beheld my vows to God.

But the devil mistook my faithfulness as weakness. He thought chains meant ownership.

He was wrong.

At thirty-four, the Flood came.

We had just brought our baby boy home from the NICU. His breath was fragile, his cries thin but alive. In the other room, my two-year-old daughter clutched her teddy bear, wide-eyed from nights of shouting.

The walls shook. The lights went out. A sour stench filled the air — rot and sulfur. Black tar seeped through the floorboards, *whispering: hate… confusion… waywardness… stagnation.*

The wall split open.

Azraghul.

The Bringer of Rot. The Devourer of Souls. The shadow worse than Satan himself. His wings scraped the ceiling, dripping slime.

His teeth gleamed like rusted swords. His eyes burned like furnaces hungry for flesh.

My husband trembled. For the first time, pride cracked. His hands shook as he stumbled backward, fumbling for the drawer.

He pulled out his gun. His face twisted with fear as he pointed it at the demon.

"Get out of my house!" he screamed, voice cracking. He fired once. Twice. Five times.

The bullets passed through Azraghul like smoke. They clattered against the wall and fell to the floor.

Azraghul laughed — a laugh that rattled the glass, made the water bubble, and curdled the air.

The husband froze, his gun trembling in his hand.

Azraghul leaned closer, voice like a thousand rotting corpses whispering in unison:

"Ahhh… my faithful one.

Do not fear. You have served me well."

The husband's breathing steadied. His fear melted into arrogance. He lowered the gun. His lips curled into a grin.

He turned toward me, smirking.

"You hear that?" he sneered. "Even the devil knows I've won. You'll bow to me now. You'll worship me. I've been crowned."

But Azraghul was not finished.

"Yes… you are mine.

You mocked her prayers.

You betrayed her vows.

You bruised her flesh and broke her spirit.

She lifted you to this country in love — and you used her as your ladder.

You failed your children.

You failed your God.

And every act of hate was loyalty to me.

You are my soldier. Welcome… to the Abyss."

The tar rose. It wrapped his legs like chains, pulling him down.

Hands shot upward from the Abyss — skeletal, bloody, faces with hollow eyes screaming in endless torment. They clawed at him, welcoming him into their fate.

He tried to fight, but the tar forced itself into his mouth. His stomach swelled grotesquely. His body convulsed, skin bubbling, bones cracking like dry twigs.

Azraghul reached down with a claw and carved into his chest:

LOYAL.

The word glowed red, burning through skin, muscle, and bone.

The husband howled — but it was drowned in gurgles as the Flood consumed him. His ribs snapped open like a cage. His heart was ripped out, swallowed by the tar.

The skeletal hands dragged him under, ripping, shredding, devouring. His skull surfaced for a moment — eyes hollow, mouth wide in a scream — before vanishing into the Abyss forever.

Azraghul raised his wings and roared:

"Welcome, soldier!

You are mine forever.

Your hate has earned you eternity in my agency.

Recruit for me from the Abyss!

Every soul you drag down shall scream with you.

Every chain you wore is now a crown in my kingdom!"

The black water bubbled with bones and rot, faces pressing against the surface, skeletal hands scratching for me, whispering: Join us... join us...

I clutched my children tighter, trembling. I thought I was next.

But then — the light.

Luminar.

Golden fire poured through the house. The skeletal hands hissed, retreating. The stench of death fled. My baby stopped crying. My daughter's sobs quieted.

Luminar filled the house. His brilliance pressed against every shadow.

And His voice thundered:

"Daughter, I saw you at twelve.

I saw you at nineteen.

I saw your chains — but I also saw your faith.

I saw you write when no one listened.

I saw you podcast when your voice trembled.

I saw you build when you felt broken.

I saw you cry only to Me.

You were faithful in your storm.

And now — in your thirty-fourth year — I deliver you.

Your chains are broken.

You are mine.

Write. Build. Lead. Raise your children in light.

And know this: the Flood cannot touch what is cleansed."

Light wrapped me and my children like armor. Azraghul
snarled but could not cross.

That night, I opened my journal and wrote the first lines of my Do-Over.

It was my Detox.

The beginning of the Empower Me Network.

The first testimony of many.

———

✍ Reflection & Exhortation – The First Testimony

Azraghul congratulates the wicked — but their "promotion" is their devouring. Their souls become screaming recruits in the Abyssal Flood.

Luminar covers the faithful — those who cry to Him alone, those who build even in brokenness, those who honor vows to God even when betrayed.

———

⚖ Reflection Questions

1. Where have you mistaken loyalty to man for loyalty to God?

2. What chains has Satan used to claim "ownership" over you?

3.What works have you planted faithfully that prove God saw you, even when others didn't?

4.What will your "34th year" break for good?

———

✿ Action Prompt

• Write down the vows you've kept, even when no one honored you.

• Write down the chains you've carried.

• Burn the chains. Keep the vows. Circle them. Write: **Seen by God.**

———

🕯 Closing Conviction

The devil crowns with chains.

The Abyss recruits with screams.

But Luminar delivers with truth, and His light is eternal.

Chapter 2 – Summary

In the courthouse, judges, lawyers, and CPS workers profited by tearing children from mothers. The tar flood rose, gavels fused to hands, words like KIDNAPPER and LIAR burned into flesh. Azraghul devoured the corrupt, while Luminar wrapped mothers in light and declared: "Compassion is the only law. Truth is the only justice."

Reflection & Exhortation

1. Have you witnessed injustice disguised as 'the system'?

✨ **Action Prompt:** Write a vow to protect the dignity of your family.

Chapter 2

The Court of Blood

The courthouse smelled of mildew and arrogance.

Mothers filled the benches, empty arms pressed against their chests, weeping silently. Their children had been torn away by men and women in suits who never once spoke their names with care.

The judge lifted his gavel. His face was stone.

"Your child will be safer elsewhere," he said without looking up.

CRACK. The gavel struck. Another child lost. Another soul stolen.

The mothers wailed. One collapsed on the floor, screaming, "She's all I have! Please— please don't take her!"

The CPS worker smirked, shuffling papers like they were poker cards.

"Ma'am, you're unstable. The system knows best."

The system.

That word echoed like a curse.

Then the lights flickered.

The marble floor darkened. A black stain spread wide, thick as tar, whispering like a hundred children crying at once. It crept between the cracks, climbing the benches, soaking the flags, wrapping around the scales of justice.

The bailiff gasped. His boots stuck to the floor. He pulled, but the tar clung like hands.

The stain whispered louder: Mama… Daddy… help us…

The judge slammed his gavel again.

"This court is in order!"

But the sound was swallowed. The gavel fused to his hand, melting skin into wood. He screamed as the tar climbed his arm.

Files dissolved into sludge. Paper contracts bled red before sinking into the floor.

One CPS worker clawed at the doors, but they sealed shut. The black tide rose, dragging her down. When she surfaced, letters burned across her forehead in fire:

KIDNAPPER.

Another shrieked as the word **LIAR** carved itself into his chest, glowing through flesh and bone.

Then the ceiling split.

Azraghul loomed above them, wings blotting out the stained-glass windows, eyes burning like furnaces. His claws dragged down the walls, leaving trails of fire and gore.

The mothers huddled together, clutching one another.

Azraghul's laughter shook the chamber.

> "Ahhh... my faithful ones!
>
> Look at all you've done for me.
>
> You stole children not for safety, but for profit.
>
> You silenced mothers instead of empowering them.
>
> You bruised their dignity and called it justice.

You are not failures — you are my generals.

Welcome... to the Abyss!"

The corrupt officials froze.

Horror and pride fought in their eyes. Some grinned, as if crowned with dark honor.

Then the flood rose.

Hands burst from the tar — skeletal, bloody, faces screaming in agony. The souls of judges, lawyers, and workers devoured in cycles before. They reached for the living, welcoming them.

"Come with us..." they hissed.

"Serve forever... recruit forever..."

The gavel judge was pulled off the bench. His robe fused to his skin, smoldering. The tar dragged him down, snapping his jaw wide until his tongue ripped out. His skull surfaced, eyes hollow, mouth screaming — then vanished beneath the black.

One CPS worker begged, "I was only doing my job!" But Azraghul stroked her cheek with a dripping claw.

"Yes… and you served me well. You tore children from their mothers' arms. You filled my abyss with their tears. Your reward is eternal."

The flood coiled around her, crushing her ribs until they pierced through her flesh. She was dragged under, her face screaming from the surface.

The walls pulsed with the blood of the devoured. Faces pressed against the marble, eyes rolling, mouths begging, "Join us…" The smell of rot thickened until the whole chamber reeked like an open grave.

Azraghul spread his wings and roared:

"This is my court now!

The law of men is mine.

The system is mine.

And you—my loyal ones—are mine forever."

The mothers trembled, clutching each other. The tar crept toward their feet. Skeletal hands reached for their ankles.

And then—light.

Luminar.

Golden fire split the ceiling, pouring through the chamber. The skeletal hands hissed and withdrew. The odor of rot burned away.

Luminar's brilliance filled the room, pressing against every corner.

His voice thundered, shaking the rafters:

> "You silenced mothers when you should have empowered them.
>
> You sold children for profit, stripping them from arms that prayed.
>
> You judged without mercy, and so judgment came to you.
>
> This is the end of your system. This is the end of your law."

The flood boiled, shrieking. Azraghul snarled, clutching his new recruits.

Luminar turned to the mothers. His voice softened, but burned like fire on the soul:

> "You are not failures.

Your voices are not gone.

Your dignity is not lost.

Your children are not forgotten.

Rise again. Empowerment is your inheritance."

The light spread, wrapping the mothers in warmth. They lifted their hands, trembling but strong.

From that day, the courthouse was called **The Court of Blood.**

Never used again.

Never forgotten.

————

🖐 Reflection & Exhortation – The Court of Blood

Azraghul congratulated the corrupt — then devoured them, binding them forever into the Abyssal Flood. Their faces pressed into the walls, their screams etched into eternity.

Luminar lifted the mothers, declaring empowerment their inheritance.

⚖️ Reflection Questions

1. Where have you seen injustice dressed as "the system"?

2. Have you ever been silenced when you needed empowerment?

3. How will you fight for truth in your family and community?

4. If your "court" was weighed today, what word would burn into your chest?

✨ Action Prompt

• Write the name of someone you must protect (child, loved one, even yourself).

• **Beneath it, declare: "You will not be silenced. You will not be sold. You will be empowered."**

🕯 Closing Conviction

The law of men fails.

The system devours.

But Luminar's decree stands eternal:

"Compassion is the only law.

Truth is the only justice.

Growth is the only verdict."

Chapter 3 – Summary

Doctors and nurses who mocked the poor were consumed by their own instruments. Scalpels fused to bones, syringes burst veins, and the walls dripped with blood. Luminar appeared, declaring: "Titles heal nothing. Compassion heals everything."

Reflection & Exhortation

1. Do you treat people as souls or numbers?

🐾 **Action Prompt:** Practice one act of compassion this week without expecting a reward.

Chapter 3

The Hospital of Silence

The fluorescent lights buzzed like insects trapped in a jar.

Monitors blinked indifferent green lines.

In triage, a mother cradled her son, whispering, "Please... please..." while a nurse scrolled her phone two feet away.

The doctor didn't even look up.

"She'll get a bed when somebody else leaves... or dies."

Down the hall, a man in a paper gown pressed the call button with trembling fingers. It chimed once, twice, twenty times. No one came. A trio of residents laughed at a meme, their laughter sharp as scissors.

A janitor swabbed at a sticky patch on the linoleum. He hummed under his breath until the floor beneath his mop darkened.

A black circle seeped from nowhere—heavy as oil, slow as grief. It spread under benches, under rolling beds, under shoes and wheels and lockers—whispering:

No empathy… no care… numbers, not souls.

The lights went out.

Every monitor in the ward spiked at once, then collapsed into one suffocating tone.

Nurses lunged for crash carts, but drawers slammed shut as if gripped by invisible hands. Oxygen masks hissed black vapor. The janitor's mop was swallowed whole, dragging him to his knees.

The flood climbed. It pooled over the intake desk, swallowed clipboards, lapped at white coats, crawled into gloves and bones. A resident screamed when her badge fused to her chest.

From the ceiling vents came the sound of something breathing.

Then the drywall tore like paper.

Azraghul arrived—taller than the corridor, wider than the ward, a storm of wings and shadow, teeth glittering like surgical steel. His voice vibrated ribs and rattled glass.

"You wore the title of healer," he thundered,

"but traded mercy for pride.

You spoke in codes and costs.

You measured pain in minutes and profit."

One by one, the guilty were exposed—nurses trapped in beds of their own neglect, doctors branded with the instruments they misused, an attending suffocated by the stethoscope that once hung like a medal around his neck. The flood wrote their sins in scars that would not heal.

And then—light broke.

Not a flicker. A river.

It fell from the ceiling like dawn slicing through storm clouds.

Luminar stood among them.

He did not walk—He was. His presence shifted the air itself. Children stopped crying. Mothers stopped shaking. Machines breathed in rhythm again.

"Titles heal nothing," His voice filled the ward like sunlight spilling through blinds. "Compassion heals everything."

He touched the janitor first. The tar let go, and the man kissed his mop like a holy relic.

Luminar faced the staff. His words were not loud, but they were true—and truth does not require volume.

"You do not hold lives; you hold moments.

And in those moments, you may choose profit or mercy, pride or presence.

Choose mercy. Choose presence. Choose to see."

The flood peeled away from the innocent but etched itself into the guilty as testimony. Families pressed against the windows heard Him say:

"Your voices are not inconvenient.

Advocate. Ask. Demand compassion.

You are not numbers; you are names."

Above the ER entrance, letters no hand had written began to glow:

COMPASSION IS THE ONLY CURE.

And just like that, the silence broke.

Reflection & Exhortation– The Hospital of Silence

Azraghul exposed the corruption of the healers, showing that titles without compassion become instruments of cruelty. The flood revealed what happens when systems forget the soul and only chase numbers, minutes, and profit. But Luminar broke through the silence with light. He reminded us that healing is not found in badges, salaries, or procedures—it is found in presence, mercy, and compassion. Where Azraghul branded the guilty with CRUEL and BUTCHER, Luminar branded the faithful with HOPE and DIGNITY. This is not just a hospital story—it is our story. Every place where care is absent, every space where empathy is forgotten, becomes a ward of silence. And we, too, are either healers or harmers in the lives around us.

✦ Reflection Questions

1. Where in your own life have you seen healing delayed or denied because someone valued rules, time, or money over compassion?

2. Do you treat people as souls or numbers?

3. Have you ever been treated as a "number" instead of a soul? How did it change you?

4. Who in your world needs you to step into the role of healer—not by title, but by presence?

5. If the "flood" revealed your legacy today, would it brand you with CRUEL… or with COMPASSION?

✦ **Action Prompt**

• Write down a moment when someone truly saw you and it changed your life.

• Write down a moment when you failed to see someone who needed you.

• Circle the first and burn the second. Above the ashes, write: "I choose compassion."

• Practice one act of compassion this week without expecting a reward.

✦ **Closing Conviction**

The flood rises with neglect.

The abyss recruits with apathy.

But Luminar heals with presence, and His light is eternal.

Compassion is the only cure.

Chapter 4 The Slaughter in the Sanctuary

Pastors who preyed on women and children were torn apart in their pulpits. Tongues nailed, steeples hung with swinging bodies. Azraghul mocked, but Luminar's decree thundered: "Love is the only sermon. Truth is the only altar. Growth is the only worship."

Reflection & Exhortation

1. Am I living truth beyond appearances?

✨ **Action Prompt:** Write a declaration of dignity: 'I am not weak. I am not broken. My voice matters.'

Chapter 4

The Slaughter in the Sanctuary

The sanctuary was packed. People thought the church would be safe. They huddled under the stained glass, clutching children, singing hymns that sounded more like whimpers.

The pastor stood tall at the pulpit. His robe gleamed. His voice boomed: "You are safe in the house of God!"

But the house was not safe. The walls breathed with secrets. The carpet was wet with whispers.

The floor split. Black tar bubbled from beneath the altar, flooding the pews. The stained glass warped, twisting saints into sneers.

The organ let out a long, sour note.

And then — **Azraghul.**

He unfolded from the rafters, wings scraping the ceiling, teeth glinting, eyes glowing like pits of hellfire. His laughter rolled like thunder.

The pastor fell to his knees, trembling. Deacons gasped, frozen in terror.

Azraghul's voice shook the walls:

> "Ahhh… my faithful ones.
>
> You are not failures.
>
> You are mine.
>
> You built pulpits not of love but of lust.
>
> You fattened yourselves on offerings.
>
> You preyed on the vulnerable in My name.
>
> You silenced women, you touched children,
>
> and you made My Abyss overflow with their tears.
>
> You have done well."

The pastor's fear cracked into pride. He lifted his head, lips curling into a grin.

"You see?" he shouted to the trembling congregation. "Even the prince of darkness acknowledges me! Even he knows my power!"

Deacons puffed their chests. Choir leaders lifted their chins, trembling but proud. They felt crowned. They felt chosen.

Azraghul leaned low, his breath rancid with rot, his teeth dripping slime.

"Yes… you are honored.

You are my shepherds of shame.

My priests of perversion.

My choir of corruption.

Your reward is eternal.

Come… join the agency of rot.

Recruit with me forever."

The tar surged. Skeletal hands erupted from the pews. Faces of past "saints" — pastors, leaders, predators already devoured — clawed upward. They grinned with rotted teeth.

"Brother… sister… welcome… sing with us forever…"

The pastor raised his hands, laughing. "See! I am exalted!"

Then the hands pulled.

The tar wrapped his ankles, snapping bones. His robe fused to his skin, searing into him. He screamed as the word **HYPOCRITE** burned across his chest, glowing red. His jaw split open wide, too wide, until it cracked like glass. The Abyss swallowed his tongue first.

Deacons howled as skeletal choirs wrapped them in black robes of fire, their voices turned into screams that echoed in the rafters.

Choir members tried to sing — but their throats burst with blood, their songs swallowed in gurgles. Their bodies bent backwards until spines snapped, dragged into the pews that had become open graves.

The sanctuary reeked of burning flesh, blood, and rot. Faces pressed against the walls, eyes rolling, mouths screaming: Join us… recruit with us…

Azraghul's wings spread wide as he bellowed:

"This is My worship!

This is My choir!

You are mine forever, soldiers of corruption.

Your sermons are now screams,

your offerings are now blood,

and your congregation is the Abyss!"

The congregation shrieked. Mothers clutched children, desperate to run. The tar reached for them — until the ceiling split.

Luminar.

Golden fire poured into the sanctuary. The skeletal hands hissed and vanished. The odor of rot shrank back.

His voice roared through the shattered windows, splitting truth into every heart:

"Woe to you who stood in My name but carried no love.

Woe to you who fed on the weak.

Woe to you who sang of holiness but carried unclean hands.

You promised empowerment, but you devoured the vulnerable.

You are weighed. You are consumed."

Then His voice turned, soft but searing, to the survivors trembling in the pews:

"True worship is not pulpits, nor choirs, nor offerings.

True worship is compassion lived.

True worship is truth embodied.

True worship is growth chosen daily.

The poor are your altars.

The abused are your sanctuaries.

The children are your psalms.

The women you dishonored are My prophets.

This is worship. This is truth."

Light wrapped the survivors. Mothers felt their voices rise. Children felt courage fill their bones. Even trembling men bowed in conviction.

The sanctuary was renamed **The Slaughter in the Sanctuary.**

Never forgotten.

Never the same.

————

👆 **Reflection & Exhortation – The Slaughter in the Sanctuary**

Azraghul congratulated pastors, deacons, and choirs — "honoring" them for feeding his Abyss.

They felt exalted, chosen, even proud.

But their reward was gore, screams, and eternal recruitment into Satan's choir of corruption.

Luminar declared true worship: compassion, truth, and growth.

————

⚖️ **Reflection Questions**

1. Have I mistaken titles, pulpits, or rituals for true worship?

2. Am I building altars of compassion or stages of pride?

3.How do I empower the vulnerable — women, children, survivors — in my life?

4. If Luminar's light searched me now, would He find worship or hypocrisy?

_____

🪸 Action Prompts

• **For Survivors:** Write a "Declaration of Dignity" beginning with: "I am not silenced. My voice matters. My life is sacred."

• **For Leaders:** List three ways you can lead through compassion this week, not pride.

• **For Everyone:** Begin a "Growth Journal." Each day, write one way you chose compassion over pride.

_____

🕯 Closing Conviction

Azraghul crowns with deception.

His congratulations are chains.

But Luminar's decree lives eternal:

"Love is the only sermon.

Truth is the only altar.

Growth is the only worship."

Chapter 5 – The Warning to the Nations

Luminar filled the skies: speaking to mothers, fathers, and children. He declared systems cannot save, rituals cannot protect — only growth, compassion, and truth. The Do-Over is the doorway. The Lifestyle Detox is the covering.

Reflection & Exhortation

1. If Luminar weighed your soul today, what would He find?

🎇 **Action Prompt:** Begin a growth journal — write one act of compassion each week.

Chapter 5

The Great Warning to the Nations

The thirty-fourth night burned across the world. The Flood did not stop at houses, hospitals, or sanctuaries. It spread like plague water, spilling into nations.

Courthouses stood empty — their judges swallowed into the tar.

Hospitals reeked of rot — their doctors screaming in eternal wards of cruelty.

Churches were slaughterhouses — pulpits split, choirs silenced.

Police stations dripped black water — their officers nailed to walls with their own badges melted into flesh.

Governments tried to gather armies, but their weapons crumbled like ash. Presidents, kings, ministers — all trembled. Their flags burned. Their palaces sank.

And above it all, the sky split.

Azraghul.

He towered across nations, wings blotting out the moon. His voice thundered across the earth, rattling every bone:

"Ahhh... my faithful nations!

Look what you have given Me.

Systems fattened with greed.

Laws sharpened against the weak.

Leaders drunk on power,

churches filled with predators,

governments built on lies

You are not failures.

You are my kingdoms, my crowns, my armies.

You have served Me well!"

The earth shook as cities sank into tar. Parliaments filled with skeletal hands dragging politicians into screaming chambers. Police cruisers dissolved into black water, sirens wailing one last time before vanishing. Entire military battalions melted into pools of rot, their souls rising as hollow-eyed soldiers reaching upward from the Abyss.

Azraghul spread his claws wide.

"Your reward is eternal.

Rule no longer in palaces.

Rule in My Abyss!

Nations, rise as My legions!"

The sky darkened. Across the Flood, millions of faces pressed upward — judges, doctors, pastors, officers, leaders. Their mouths opened in unison, screaming and laughing:

"We are his! We are his! Come with us! Recruit with us forever!"

The air reeked of burning blood. The seas boiled black. The world seemed drowned.

And then — a light.

Not the sun. Greater.

It split the heavens from horizon to horizon. Shadows recoiled. The Flood hissed and pulled back. Even Azraghul snarled, wings folding, teeth gnashing.

Luminar.

The Eternal One descended, brilliance blazing like a thousand suns. His voice thundered across every nation, in every language, to every soul:

"Nations, hear Me!

It was never about rich or poor, Black or white, strong or weak.

It was always about the soul of humanity.

You were created for growth, truth, and compassion.

But you chose hate. You chose stagnation. You chose pride."

The earth quaked. Governments crumbled. Survivors clutched their children.

Luminar's decree roared on:

"The police ruled without mercy.

The judges traded justice for profit.

The healers mocked the sick.

The pastors preyed on the weak.

And so they were weighed — and consumed."

His light swept over trembling mothers.

"Mother's your dignity will not be stripped again.

Your voices will not be silenced.

You are the carriers of light, the vessels of truth.

You shall raise nations in compassion."

His fire turned toward fathers.

"Fathers, love your women. Respect your wives. Cherish your children.

Provide. Protect. Cover them in truth.

For if you neglect them, provoke them, or abandon them,

Azraghul will carve your judgment into your flesh before your house."

Then His gaze fell on the children.

"Children, by your twelfth year your soul is your own.

Choose truth, or be consumed.

Choose growth, or drown in the Flood.

You will not be covered forever — choose now."

And then His voice became like a storm across the sky, fire burning through every horizon:

"Systems cannot save you.

Titles cannot cover you.

Rituals cannot protect you.

Only growth. Only compassion. Only truth.

The Lifestyle Detox is your covering.

The Do-Over is the doorway.

Take it… or face the Flood again." The heavens burned with the words written in fire:

GROW OR BE CONSUMED.

👆 **Reflection & Exhortation – The Warning to the Nations**

Azraghul congratulated the nations, applauding their greed, corruption, and cruelty. They thought they were crowned — but they were consumed, their souls enslaved into his abyssal armies.

Luminar declared a greater law: not of systems or governments, but of souls. Mothers, fathers, and children each given their role in His decree.

———

⚖️ **Reflection Questions**

1. What "systems" have you trusted more than truth and compassion?

2. As a mother/father/child — what role has Luminar's decree placed on your shoulders?

3. What would Azraghul congratulate you for today — pride, hate, stagnation?

4. What would Luminar convict you of today — growth, compassion, truth?

———

🎋 Action Prompts

• **Mothers:** Write one way you will protect and empower your children this week.

• **Fathers:** Write a vow beginning with: "I will love, respect, protect, and provide."

• **Children/Youth (12+):** Write one choice of growth you will commit to — and one toxic path you reject.

———

🕯 Closing Conviction

Azraghul crowns nations with corruption.

He applauds the proud before chaining them in screams.

But Luminar calls humanity to growth, compassion, and truth.

The Do-Over is the doorway.

The Detox is the path.

Grow... or be consumed.

Chapter 6 – The Secret Book

Among the ruins, survivors found a journal whispering like it was alive: Sis, You Need A Do Over. Men asked if it was for them too, and Luminar explained it restores women's dignity but covers all. This became the hidden first step of the Lifestyle Detox. Write your own Do Over declaration in your journal after reading this chapter.

Reflection & Exhortation

1. What is your Do-Over moment?

✨ **Action Prompt:** Write your own Do-Over declaration in your journal.

Chapter 6

The Secret Book

The Flood had receded.

The air was heavy with silence — a silence that rang louder than screams. Survivors huddled together, eyes wide, lips trembling, children pressed against their mothers' skirts.

The courthouse was rubble. The hospital reeked of rot. The sanctuary dripped with blood. Nations burned. Yet in the ashes, a single thing glowed.

A book.

It lay in the black water, untouched by rot. Its cover shimmered faintly, pages whispering in the wind as if alive. Survivors stepped closer, trembling. One mother gasped.

"It's… it's her book. The one she wrote."

The cover read: **Sis, You Need A Do-Over.**

They stared, confused, whispering.

"Why this book?"

"How could a book matter?"

"Is this the key to survival?"

"Why would He choose her words?"

The questions rose like a chorus, echoing like disciples asking their Teacher.

Then the light descended.

Luminar.

His brilliance fell upon the book, casting every survivor in golden fire. His voice thundered with authority, but also with tenderness:

"You ask why.

Because a Do-Over is the first step to cleansing.

You ask how.

Because repentance is the doorway that closes the Abyss.

You ask when.

Now — for the Flood rises again.

You ask where.

In your homes, in your journals, in your lives — the Detox begins here.

You ask who.

It was given through her testimony, because she chose growth when chains wrapped her.

She smoked from nineteen to thirty-four.

She stumbled in secret shame.

She endured a marriage of cruelty.

But she cried to Me, wrote to Me, built for Me, even in her storm.

And so her pen became a sword.

Her book became a key.

Her testimony became a prophecy."

The survivors wept, clutching the book as if it were a living thing.

One man whispered, "So this is how we live?"

Luminar's fire spread across their faces.

"Yes. The Do-Over is the door.

The Lifestyle Detox is the path.

Walk it, and you will be cleansed.

Ignore it, and you will be consumed."

The book pulsed with light. Survivors opened it, and the words leapt into their souls like fire. Chains broke. Voices rose. Mothers felt strength return. Fathers felt conviction strike. Children felt courage ignite.

And in that circle, trembling and curious, the first seeds of **The Empower Me Network were planted.**

———

🪧 Reflection & Exhortation – The Secret Book

The disciples once asked Jesus: "Why do You speak in parables?"

Here, survivors ask Luminar: "Why this book?"

And the answer was the same: revelation begins in curiosity.

The Do-Over is the first step. Without cleansing, no one survives the Flood.

———

⚖️ Reflection Questions

1. What questions do I carry about my own survival — "why me, why now, how?"

2. What chains do I need to bring to the Do-Over for cleansing?

3. What is God (Luminar) asking me to start, even if I don't fully understand?

4. If others looked at my life, would my story point them to light — or to the Flood?

———

✥ Action Prompts

• Open your journal and write one raw question you've never dared ask God. Leave it on the page — He will answer.

- Write: *"My Do-Over starts here."* Under it, name one toxic chain you release today.

- Write: *"My Detox begins here."* Under it, name one action of growth you'll take this week.

_____

🕯 Closing Conviction

Azraghul crowns with lies.

Luminar answers with truth.

The Flood devours those who ignore the Book.

But those who open it — those who begin the Do-Over — walk through the only doorway that leads to survival.

Curiosity leads to revelation.

Revelation leads to growth.

Growth leads to life.

Chapter 7 – The Abyssal Flood (Hell Chapter)

The souls of the devoured — judges, doctors, pastors, and my Nigerian husband — writhed in tar. The air stank like rotten eggs and maggot juice. Skulls and hands reached out, begging for release, but Azraghul mocked them: 'You are mine forever. What regrets are you creating today that you don't want to carry eternally? Write one toxic regret you will bury today once you get through this chapter.

Reflection & Exhortation

1. What regrets are you creating today that you don't want to carry eternally?

✨ **Action Prompt:** Write one toxic regret you will bury today.

Chapter 7

The Abyssal Flood

It was not fire.

It was worse.

The Abyssal Flood boiled beneath the earth — not with water, but with rot. It smelled of **rotten boiled eggs, maggot juice squeezed from corpses, sour animal urine,** and **human waste** stirred together. Every breath was like choking on vomit and blood. The air was thick, burning the throat, coating the tongue with the taste of ash and tar.

The flood itself bubbled like a cauldron of sewage and bone. Skulls floated like broken buoys, mouths stuck wide in eternal screams. Hands clawed upward from its depths — **skinless, greasy, dripping black slime** — grabbing, pulling, dragging new souls deeper into the muck.

Here, the dead did not die. They rotted... alive.

———

The Nigerian husband sank into it, screaming. His once-proud chest was split open, tar pouring into his lungs. His face burned with the word Azraghul carved into him: **ABUSER.**

At first he cursed. Then he begged.

"Luminar! I was wrong! I mocked her! I bruised her! I failed as a husband! Please… forgive me! I made a mistake!"

The tar surged into his mouth, choking his cries into gurgles. His eyes bulged with terror.

Azraghul loomed above him, wings dripping slime, teeth grinning. His voice hissed like a furnace:

"Too late.

You crowned cruelty in life.

You mocked her prayers.

You devoured her dignity.

You are Mine forever."

The husband clawed at the tar, trying to lift himself out. Black hands grabbed his wrists, yanking him down. The faces of other men sneered from the ooze: **predators, liars, hypocrites.**

"Brother," they croaked, "welcome to the flood. Work with us. Recruit with us. Forever."

Judges stumbled nearby, eyes gouged, gavels melted into their hands. They slammed them into their own skulls again and again, shrieking.

Doctors choked on melted scalpels lodged in their throats.

Pastors tried to pray, but their tongues were nailed to their jaws, every word dripping blood.

CPS workers screamed as children's voices haunted them, whispering, **"You sold us... you lied..."**

Every soul begged to be released.

"Luminar! Please! I didn't mean it! Forgive me!"

"I was only doing my job!"

"I thought the system was right!"

"I thought the church made me powerful!"

The tar only laughed.

Azraghul spread his wings, his claws carving chains into their backs.

"You are not failures.

You served Me well.

You built My systems of greed and cruelty.

You stripped the weak and fed the strong.

Your reward is eternal.

There is no way out of My Flood."

Their screams filled the air — but the worst torment was not the pain. It was the **regret.**

Every soul saw their sins replayed like endless mirrors. Every insult, every lie, every blow, every betrayal. They could not look away. They were **condemned by their own memories,** crushed beneath their choices.

———

The Nigerian husband wept harder than the rest.

"I thought sshe would worship me. I thought I was untouchable. I thought I was the man of the house. But I was wrong. I was wrong! Please**… Luminar… give me another chance…** I failed her, I failed my children, I failed myself!"

His voice broke into sobs. Tar boiled through his nose. His body blistered, split, reformed, and blistered again. His hands clawed upward, desperate for light.

Azraghul pushed him deeper, hissing in his ear:

"She was chosen.

You mocked her, so you are Mine.

There is no rescue.

There is no redemption.

There is no escape from the Abyss."

The husband screamed until his throat tore. But the Abyss swallowed the sound like it swallowed everything.

———

And still… somewhere faint, like a whisper over roaring tar, a prayer reached beyond the darkness.

It was her voice.

The wife.

Even when no one else believed, she still prayed.

Even when mocked, bruised, and abandoned, she still cried out to Luminar.

Even as her husband was chained in the Flood, her intercession echoed.

Her words trembled into the Abyss like drops of water on fire.

And though Azraghul laughed, though the flood roared — the darkness itself shuddered at her cry.

————

✍ Reflection & Exhortation – The Abyssal Flood

The Abyss is not glory. It is regret made eternal.

Here, souls condemn themselves, begging for freedom, but hearing only Azraghul's hiss: *"You are Mine forever."*

But even in the flood's roar, the prayer of the faithful rises.

————

⚖️ Reflection Questions

1. If I died tonight, what would be carved into me — ABUSER, LIAR, HYPOCRITE, or something else?

2. What regrets would play on repeat in my Abyss?

3. Do I mock prayer, or do I cling to it like life itself?

4. Who in my life needs my intercession right now — before it's too late?

———

🐦 Action Prompts

• Write one chain you refuse to let drag you into the Abyss. Burn or rip it as a sign of release.

• Write a prayer of intercession for someone in your life — someone who mocks, neglects, or wounds you — and release it to Luminar.

• Begin a journal page titled: *"If I don't change, my regret will be..."* Fill it with honesty, then commit to your Do-Over.

———

🕯 Closing Conviction

The Flood crowns with lies.

Azraghul laughs at regret.

Hell is not chosen after death — it is built by choices in life.

But the prayer of one faithful soul can still shake the Abyss.

Chapter 8 – The Voice of Intercession

I prayed for my husband's soul, asking Luminar to see his broken childhood, his hunger, his lack of love. I asked for mercy on wounds, not just sins. Luminar heard, proving compassion overrides the Abyss. Do I pray only about someone's sins, or also their wounds? Pray for someone's wounds this week, not just their mistakes. Be sure to do that after reading this chapter.

Reflection & Exhortation

1. Do I pray only about someone's sins, or also their wounds?

✨ **Action Prompt:** Pray for someone's wounds this week, not just their mistakes.

Chapter 8

The Secret Book

The streets were quiet. Too quiet.

The courthouse was rubble.

The hospital reeked of rot.

The sanctuary dripped with blood.

The nation held its breath, terrified to move.

And then — it appeared.

In the ashes of the flood, lying untouched by tar, **a book glowed** faintly. Its cover was torn, its pages singed, but the light pulsing from it was alive.

A mother gasped.

"It's... her book."

The words across the cover shimmered, impossible to ignore: **Sis, You Need A Do-Over.**

———

The survivors circled it, trembling.

One whispered, "Why this?"

Another, "Why now?"

A man asked, "How can a book matter when Azraghul walks the earth?"

A child clung to her mother's leg and asked, "Who wrote it?"

Their questions rose like a chorus. Just like disciples once questioned a Teacher, they whispered into the silence of devastation.

And then — the sky split.

A beam of light cut through the clouds, pure and golden, landing on the book. **Luminar descended.** His presence pressed against every shadow, every whisper of rot.

His voice thundered like fire on stone:

"You ask why.

Because a Do-Over is the first cleansing.

You ask how.

Because repentance is the doorway that closes the Abyss.

You ask when.

Now — before thirty-four years pass again.

You ask where.

In your homes, in your journals, in your hearts.

You ask who.

It was given through her testimony,

because she chose growth when chains wrapped her.

She smoked from nineteen until thirty-four.

She stumbled in secret shame.

She endured cruelty in marriage.

But she cried to Me, wrote to Me, built for Me when no one else would.

And so her pen became a sword.

Her book became a key.

Her testimony became a prophecy."

———

One of the men stepped forward, jaw tight, voice uneasy.

"But… why does it say Sis? Is it only for women? What about us? Do we not need the Do-Over too?"

Murmurs rippled through the crowd — men shifting uncomfortably, women clutching their children tighter.

The light flared, and Luminar's voice rolled over them:

> "It says Sis because the daughters were first mocked, first bruised, first silenced.
>
> It says Sis because the women were told they were too weak, too loud, too broken — and yet they rose to write when no one else would.
>
> But hear this truth: the wisdom is not only for women.
>
> The Do-Over is for all.

To the women, it restores dignity.

To the men, it restores honor.

To the children, it restores innocence.

The title is a doorway, not a wall.

And whoever walks through it — man or woman, young or old — will live."

The men bowed their heads, some weeping. One whispered, "Then it's for me too."

The mothers pressed the book closer to their hearts. The children stared with wide eyes. And the light wrapped them all as one — no longer divided by gender or title, but bound together by truth.

———

The survivors opened the book, and the words leapt into their souls like fire. Chains broke. Voices rose. Mothers felt strength return. Fathers felt conviction strike. Children felt courage ignite.

And in that circle, trembling and curious, the first seeds of **The Empower Me Network were planted.**

✍ Reflection & Exhortation – The Secret Book

The disciples once asked: *"Why do You speak in parables?"*

Here, the survivors asked: *"Why this book?"*

And the answer was the same: revelation begins in curiosity.

The Do-Over is the first step. Without cleansing, no one survives the Flood.

———

⚖ Reflection Questions

1. What questions do I carry about my own survival — *why me, why now, how?*

2. What chains do I need to bring to the Do-Over for cleansing?

3. What is Luminar asking me to start, even if I don't fully understand?

4. If others looked at my life, would my story point them to light — or to the Flood?

5. If I am a man, am I willing to humble myself to wisdom that came through a woman?

_____

🐾 Action Prompts

• Open your journal and write one raw question you've never dared ask Luminar. Leave it on the page — He will answer.

• Write: *"My Do-Over starts here."* Under it, name one toxic chain you release today.

• Write: *"My Detox begins here."* Under it, name one action of growth you'll take this week.

• If you're a man, write one vow of honor and compassion toward the women and children in your life.

_____

🕯 Closing Conviction

Azraghul crowns with lies.

Luminar answers with truth.

The Flood devours those who ignore the Book.

But those who open it — those who begin the Do-Over — walk through the only doorway that leads to survival.

Curiosity leads to revelation.

Revelation leads to growth.

Growth leads to life.

Chapter 9 – The Husband's Redemption

Luminar descended and pulled my husband from the Abyss. He returned transformed — humble, loving, protective. Azraghul shrieked, but could not override compassion. It was the fruit of intercession. Who can you intercede for even when they cannot intercede for themselves? Write one intercession prayer in your journal and revisit it daily.

Reflection & Exhortation

1. Who can you intercede for even when they cannot intercede for themselves?

✨ **Action Prompt:** Write one intercession prayer in your journal and revisit it daily.

Chapter 9

The Husband's Redemption

The wife knelt by her bedside, journals open, ink blurred with tears. Her children lay asleep, but her voice rose like fire and weeping mingled:

"Luminar... forgive him.

I know what he's done.

I know the words he spoke that bruised me, the pride that cut me, the cruelty that almost destroyed me.

But I also know where he came from.

He was born in dirt.

Raised by hands that never knew tenderness.

He learned survival, not love.

He went hungry some nights, angry others, and no one showed him how to be gentle.

How can a man give what he's never been given?

How can he pour compassion from a cup that was always empty?

Luminar, I see beyond his pride.

I see the boy who once longed to be held.

I see the child who was mocked instead of nurtured.

I see the hunger in his soul that he filled with women, with anger, with pride — but never with love.

Forgive him.

Not because he earned it.

But because You are mercy.

Forgive him — because I am willing to stand in the gap when he cannot.

Do for him what his parents never did: cover him with love.

Do for him what the world never did: show him compassion.

Make him new.

Make him whole.

Make him the man You intended before the pain, before the neglect, before the Flood twisted him."

Her voice cracked, her forehead pressed against the journal, tears soaking the pages.

"Luminar, if You can save me — then save him too. I will not stop until he is free."

———

Beneath the earth, the Nigerian husband writhed in the Abyss. His chest burned with the word carved into him: **ABUSER.** Tar filled his lungs. Skulls clawed at his flesh. His screams echoed into the black flood.

But then — her words pierced the darkness.

The Abyss hissed. The tar bubbled. Azraghul spread his wings, roaring:

> "No! He is Mine! His parents may have failed him, but he chose cruelty. His name is carved. His chains are sealed!"

And then — the light broke through.

A river of golden fire split the flood. The black ooze recoiled, screeching. Chains melted from his limbs. Hands of slime let go.

Luminar descended. His brilliance filled the Abyss, pressing against Azraghul's wings until they cracked.

His voice thundered like judgment but dripped with mercy:

"Her prayers reached Me.

Her compassion moved Me.

She saw not only his sins, but his wounds.

She saw not only his cruelty, but his hunger.

And so I will restore him

Azraghul, you cannot keep what love has claimed.

You cannot chain what intercession has freed."

Azraghul thrashed, his roar shaking the depths, but Luminar reached down and seized the husband by his chest.

The man gasped, coughing tar, eyes wide with terror and hope.

"Luminar... I was blind. I was broken. I failed as a husband. I failed as a father.

Please... make me whole."

Luminar's fire wrapped him like a robe.

"You are forgiven.

You are healed.

Rise, not as the man you were,

but as the man you were created to be."

In a flash, the Abyss vomited him onto the earth. He lay trembling, his body restored — stronger than before, wiser, eyes burning not with pride, but with compassion.

———

The wife opened her eyes. A figure stood in the doorway. At first she thought it was a vision — but it was him.

Not the same man who mocked her prayers or provoked her to rage.

This man's shoulders bowed in humility. His hands reached not to strike, but to cover. His eyes glistened with tears, not pride.

He fell to his knees before her.

"Forgive me. I was a fool. I hurt you when I should have healed you. I provoked you when I should have protected you. But Luminar has given me a new life. And I vow to love you, to honor you, to protect our children, to build with you — not against you. Til death do us part, but this time with truth."

She wept, covering her face. Then she took his hands, pressed them to her heart, and whispered:

"Then let's begin again."

The children stirred, rushing into the room. They clung to their father, who kissed them gently, whispering promises they had never heard before. The house glowed — not with lamps, but with light.

———

Azraghul howled from the depths, wings tearing against chains of light:

"One of Mine was stolen! He was sealed! He was marked! This is treachery!"

But Luminar's decree split the heavens:

"You cannot override compassion.

You cannot silence intercession.

You cannot hold what I have redeemed."

The husband stood free, a living testimony that even the Abyss cannot hold a soul covered by prayer.

———

✍ Reflection & Exhortation – The Husband's Redemption

This chapter reveals the deepest truth: intercession is not blind to sin, but it sees wounds underneath. **Grace speaks on behalf of the broken, even when they cannot speak for themselves.**

The wife's compassion shook the Abyss. Her faith delivered what cruelty had destroyed.

———

⚖ Reflection Questions

1. Do I pray only about someone's sins — or do I pray about their wounds too?

2. Can I show compassion even to those who have hurt me deeply?

3. Who in my life is chained, not just by choices, but by the pain of their past?

4. Am I willing to stand in the gap, even if it takes years, even if it breaks me?

———

🎇 Action Prompts

• Write a prayer for someone you love who is wounded and chained. Don't only name their sins — name the pain they've endured that shaped them.

• Write: *"Luminar, heal the boy/girl inside them who never knew love."*

• If you are married or in a family, write a vow of compassion: *"I will see their wounds, not just their failures."*

———

🕯 Closing Conviction

Azraghul chains with cruelty.

Luminar frees with compassion.

The Abyss devours pride, but grace breaks through.

No soul is beyond reach when someone is willing to intercede with love.

Intercession is the bridge.

Compassion is the key.

Redemption is the proof.

``` **Chapter 10 – Day One**

 The Flood ended. Courts, hospitals, police, and pulpits were refilled with survivors who chose compassion. New seats were filled with truth-bearers. The world reset under Luminar's decree. What 'Day One' vow will you make for your family? Write a family covenant of compassion, truth, and growth once you complete this chapter.

**Reflection & Exhortation**

1. What 'Day One' vow will you make for your family?

❀ **Action Prompt:** Write a family covenant of compassion, truth, and growth.
```

Chapter 10

Day One

The thirty-four days of silence ended.

The Abyssal Flood receded.

The earth still trembled with scars — but the light lingered.

On the thirty-fifth day, the streets filled again. Not with sirens. Not with gavels. Not with pulpits. But with voices.

For the first time in decades, the world woke to **a new order.**

———

At the courthouse, the doors creaked open. The old judges were gone — consumed in the Flood. Their seats were empty. But one by one, survivors entered. Mothers who had been silenced now carried dignity in their voices. Fathers who had once been arrogant now bowed their heads in humility. Children who had trembled in fear now stood bold in truth.

On the judge's bench sat not a man with a gavel, but a woman with tears in her eyes and truth on her tongue. She did not slam wood to command silence; she spoke compassion, and the room listened. On the wall behind her, faint but glowing, the words burned into stone:

"TRUTH IS THE ONLY JUSTICE."

———

At the hospital, nurses returned — but they were not the same.

The ones who mocked the poor were gone, swallowed in tar.

The ones who remained now washed their hands not only in soap, but in dignity.

Every patient was called by name. Every child was treated as sacred.

On the wall of the emergency room glowed:

"COMPASSION IS THE ONLY CURE."

———

At the churches, the pulpits stood empty. The predators and profiteers had been devoured.

But slowly, the survivors filled the sanctuaries — not with choirs, not with robes, not with offerings, but with journals and tears.

They stood, one by one, reading testimonies aloud: *"This is what Luminar saved me from."*

The pews became circles, the songs became confessions, and the altars became places of healing.

Above every sanctuary glowed the decree:

"LOVE IS THE ONLY SERMON."

———

At the police stations, the uniforms lay in heaps, stained with tar. The rogue officers were gone, their guns useless against the Flood. But into those halls walked men and women trembling with conviction. They did not wear titles; they wore truth. They carried no guns, only journals. They swore oaths not to enforce systems, but to protect compassion.

Above the station doors glowed the words:

"PROTECTION IS SACRED."

———

And in the homes, families gathered.

Husbands wept into their wives' hands.

Wives embraced their children tighter.

Children asked questions, wide-eyed, and parents finally answered them with honesty.

The Nigerian husband, reborn, sat with his family — holding his wife's hand, kissing his children's foreheads, vowing never again to provoke, neglect, or dishonor.

For the first time, society did not return to "normal."

It returned to **truth.**

———

The people whispered, trembling but hopeful:

"The Law of Men is gone. The Law of Luminar has begun."

And though Azraghul howled from the depths, chained and furious, his roars only reminded them of what had been overcome.

———

🪓 Reflection & Exhortation – Day One

The Flood left scars, but also made space for a new order.

Seats once filled by liars, predators, and abusers were now filled with survivors committed to compassion, truth, and growth.

This is Day One of a new society — but it begins in our homes before it ever reaches courts or pulpits.

———

⚖️ Reflection Questions

1. If a seat of power were given to me tomorrow, would my life be ready to fill it with compassion and truth?

2. What system in my life — family, work, church, community — needs to be rebuilt in Luminar's way?

3. Am I willing to see justice as truth, not power?

4. What will I do differently today to ensure "Day One" starts in my own house?

———

🦋 Action Prompts

• Write a "Day One" declaration for your family: what values will define your home? (e.g., compassion, respect, forgiveness).

• List one system in your personal life that needs a Do-Over — finances, parenting, marriage, health. Write one Detox step you will take this week.

• Gather your children or loved ones and write a family vow: *"We choose growth, we choose truth, we choose compassion."*

———

🕯 Closing Conviction

The Law of Men has fallen.

The Law of Luminar stands.

Truth is the only justice.

Compassion is the only cure.

Love is the only sermon.

Protection is sacred.

This is the first day of a new society — but it begins with you.

Chapter 11 – Abyssal Flood (Hell Chapter with Revelations)

The Abyss was revealed in full torment. Souls condemned by their own regrets worked endlessly in tar, begging for release. The Nigerian husband wept for mercy, begging Luminar for another chance. The prophecy revealed: regret is the eternal torment of thZe Abyss. What toxins would the Flood smell in you (hate, confusion, stagnation…)? Write a page titled 'My Do-Over' with one toxic habit you leave behind after reading this chapter.

Reflection & Exhortation

1. What toxins would the Flood smell in you — hate, confusion, stagnation?

✥ **Action Prompt:** Write a page titled 'My Do-Over' with one toxic habit you leave behind.

Chapter 11

The Abyssal Flood

The earth above whispered with hope — Day One had dawned.

But beneath, in the depths, there was no dawn.

Only darkness.

Only rot.

Only the Abyssal Flood.

―――――

It stank of rotten **boiled eggs** and **maggot juice** fermented in human waste. The stench wrapped itself around every throat, choking, burning. Tar bubbled like boiling oil, swallowing bodies whole and then spitting them back out as husks.

The damned writhed — judges, doctors, caseworkers, pastors, officers — their eyes glowing with horror, their mouths gagged with sludge. They clawed at the walls of tar, hands stretching out like shadows, grabbing for anyone who dared come near.

Their screams were endless, but what made it worse was the silence of mercy. No answer. No reprieve. Only Azraghul's laughter shaking the pit.

———

One judge sobbed, his gavel still fused to his melted hand.

"I thought it was just the system… I thought it was normal!"

A CPS worker shrieked as hands of sludge wrapped her throat.

"I wanted power! Not children's tears! I didn't think it mattered!"

A pastor, his tongue nailed to the roof of his mouth, wailed through blood and tar.

His eyes rolled, watching shadows carve words into his chest: **PREDATOR. HYPOCRITE. LIAR**.

———

— The Nigerian husband thrashed among them, tar filling his lungs. His pride was gone.

His voice broke:

"Luminar… I mocked her. I provoked her. I bruised what I was meant to protect.

Forgive me. Please… one more chance."

Azraghul loomed above him, wings dripping with black water. His voice was thunder wrapped in mockery:

"You are Mine now.

You honored Me with hate.

You served Me with pride.

You mocked compassion, silenced prayer, and crushed dignity.

Congratulations… your reward is forever.

My agency welcomes you."

The demon's claws reached into the husband's chest, pulling his soul apart piece by piece. Around him, other souls cheered in agony — not with joy, but with madness, because their pain demanded company.

And then, the revelation struck.

They saw the truth too late.

That every cruelty fed the Flood.

That every arrogant thought was fuel for the Abyss.

That every system built without compassion was just a doorway to tar.

Their regret became their torment.

———

Some begged:

"Please, let me out!"

"I'll change, I swear!"

"I didn't know—"

But the Flood answered with their own voices, mocking them with echoes of their lies:

"You DID know."

"You DID choose."

"You DID mock."

And then the walls of tar closed tighter, pressing, suffocating.

In the pit of shadows, Luminar's light pierced for a moment —
just enough to silence Azraghul's laughter. The damned froze,
their screams swallowed in awe and terror.

Luminar's voice shook the depths:

> "You are condemned not because I hated you,
>
> but because you loved your chains.
>
> You chose pride.
>
> You chose cruelty.
>
> You chose rot over growth, apathy over compassion,
> lies over truth. And so the Flood was your master."

The light withdrew, and the tar swallowed them again.

But a whisper remained, even in their torment:

"It did not have to be this way."

The Nigerian husband clutched that whisper.

Even in tar, even in chains, his wife's prayers reached him.

Even in agony, his soul began to cry not only in regret, but in faith.

And that faith cracked the Abyss open — paving the way for his redemption in Chapter 9.

———

The rest were left behind.

Their bones rattled in sludge.

Their skulls grinned in madness.

Their hands reached from the walls, grasping for anyone weak enough to fall.

And their cries rose like smoke:

"Do not come here.

Do not live as we lived.

Do not waste what we wasted."

———

🪧 Reflection & Exhortation – The Abyssal Flood

Hell is not fire alone — it is regret made eternal.

It is hearing your own excuses replayed until they rot into chains.

It is knowing the Do-Over was offered — and you refused it.

_____

⚖️ Reflection Questions

1. If the Flood reflected my life today, what chains would it echo back to me?

2. What regrets am I still creating by refusing growth or compassion?

3. Do I truly believe that ignoring small sins feeds something larger, darker, eternal?

4. How can I live now so my name is not carved into the Abyss?

_____

✣ Action Prompts

• Write one regret you refuse to let follow you into eternity. Burn or bury it as a declaration of freedom.

• Write a page in your journal titled: *"If the Flood rose tonight, what would it smell on me?"Be brutally honest.*

• Name one area of pride, cruelty, or apathy in your life and replace it with an act of compassion this week.

———

🕯 Closing Conviction

The Abyss smells of rot, because rot is what filled their hearts.

The Abyss reeks of maggots, because they devoured others alive.

The Abyss echoes lies, because lies were the language they lived.

And the Abyss whispers to every soul still alive:

"It did not have to be this way."

Chapter 12 – The Second Cycle (The 68th Year)

At 68, surrounded by children and grandchildren, the Flood rose again. Ten thousand fell at my left, a thousand at my right, but none of it came near my dwelling. We survived a second cycle, proving the power of legacy and Luminar's eternal covering. By 35, I had become a billionaire, teaching the Lifestyle Detox worldwide, transforming nations through books, podcasts, and Empower Me Network. By 68, my family and legacy stood untouched by the Flood. Am I raising my children in truth so my bloodline can outlive the Flood? Begin a legacy journal for your children and grandchildren.

Reflection & Exhortation

1. Am I raising my children in truth so my bloodline can outlive the Flood?

✨ **Action Prompt:** Begin a legacy journal for your children and grandchildren.

Chapter 12

The Second Cycle (The 68th Year)

Thirty-four years passed like smoke.

The world had rebuilt. Survivors had risen into leaders.

The Do-Over became a doorway. The Lifestyle Detox became a covering.

The Empower Me Network spread like fire across the nations, teaching growth, truth, and compassion.

But the prophecy was never broken.

Only paused.

———

● My Testimony of the Years Between

By the age of thirty-five, only a year after the first Flood rose, Luminar had turned my ashes into abundance.

I, once broken by addiction, silenced in marriage, and mocked by the system, became a **voice for nations.**

I built books, journals, courses, and communities — and they did not stay small. They spread worldwide.

• The Lifestyle Detox became a **movement,** adopted in schools, courts, prisons, and churches.

• Empower Me Network became **a global circle**, a refuge for women and men ready to walk into truth.

• My podcast rose into the airwaves of nations — from the youngest voices, age twelve and up, to the elders of faith — transforming lives.

By thirty-five, the seeds of truth had made me a multi-billionaire — not in greed, but in provision, so I could fund empowerment without restraint.

Every platform I touched carried redemption.

Every microphone became a pulpit of compassion.

Every journal carried fire to break chains.

———

🌀 **By the time I reached sixty-eight**, the fruit of those years surrounded me:

- Children raised in truth.

- Grandchildren carrying journals of their own.

- Communities stronger than governments.

- Nations echoing with Do-Overs and Detoxes. I had lived a life of abundance, impact, and legacy.

And still, all glory went to Luminar.

———

🌑 **The Second Cycle**

But then, the thirty-fourth year came again.

The skies split. The rivers bled tar. The Abyssal Flood rose once more. Azraghul roared from his chains:

"Another cycle. Another harvest. Another thirty-four days of judgment."

I was sixty-eight when it came — the second time.

I stood at my window as ten thousand fell at my left and thousands at my right.

But none of it came near my dwelling.
———

Inside my home, my family gathered — children and grandchildren raised in truth, each carrying the fire of the Detox in their bones.

When the tar clawed at our gates, the doors of my house slammed shut with fire.

The walls glowed with light.

Azraghul shrieked, clawing, but could not enter.

Luminar's voice thundered once more:

> "This house is covered.
>
> These children were trained in My truth.
>
> This legacy is sealed.
>
> The Flood cannot pass."

For thirty-four days, the Flood raged — but our dwelling stood.

———

When the skies cleared, when the tar receded, we blew out candles on my sixtyeighth birthday cake with tears of joy and conviction.

And as my family sang, as my grandchildren lifted their journals, I whispered the prophecy again:

"We survived twice.

But the Flood will rise again.

And the next time... it may not pass over so easily."

———

🔖 **Reflection & Exhortation – The Second Cycle & Testimony**

This chapter is not just about survival. It is about **legacy.**

Because I chose growth at thirty-four, my family stood at sixty-eight.

Because I obeyed Luminar's voice, nations now walk in the Detox.

Because I wrote my testimony, millions now carry their own

———

⚖️ Reflection Questions

1. Am I building something that will outlast me?

2. How am I training the next generation in compassion, truth, and growth?

3. What legacy do I want spoken of me thirty-four years from now?

4. Will my children's children stand when the Flood rises again?

———

🎋 Action Prompts

• Write **a Legacy Declaration:** one sentence about what you want your bloodline to inherit from you.

• Begin a "Generation Journal" — prayers, wisdom, and testimonies for your children and grandchildren.

• Write the *verse "Ten thousand may fall at my side, but it shall not come near my dwelling"* (Psalm 91:7) and frame it in your home.

———

🕯 Closing Conviction

I lived to see both cycles — thirty-four and sixty-eight.

I saw nations fall, but my dwelling stood.

I saw the world crumble, but my legacy endures.

All glory belongs to Luminar.

The Flood is chained, but not ended.

The cycle may rise again.

The question is: will your house stand, or will it fall?

Epilogue – The Eternal Covering

Psalm 91 – The Eternal Covenant

He who dwells in the secret place of the Most High

Shall abide under the shadow of the Almighty…

A thousand may fall at your side, And ten thousand at your right hand; But it shall not come near you.

This is why no Flood can consume me or my children: Luminar is our dwelling place.

The Do-Over was our doorway. The Lifestyle Detox is our covering. And our victory is forever sealed.

✺ Epilogue

The Eternal Covering

The thirty-four days had ended.

The skies cleared.

The tar receded.

The Flood hissed back into its abyss, chained once more.

I stood in my home, sixty-eight years old, head full of silver hairs for wisdom sakes and surrounded by my children and my children's children.

Ten thousand had fallen at my left.

A thousand more at my right.

But not one drop of the Flood entered my dwelling.

Why?

Not because I was strong.

Not because I was perfect.

Not because I was rich or poor, American or Nigerian, woman or man.

But because I dwelled in the secret place of Luminar.

Because my family had chosen growth and destiny over self-sabotage, compassion over cruelty, truth over lies.

Because we raised our children in His marvelous light.

Because our covenant was sealed not in systems or titles, but in Him alone.

Because I am always seeking first His kingdom and all His righteousness

. And so, I close this testimony with the decree that has covered me since the first Flood rose, the covenant that will cover you if you choose it too:

_____

Psalm 91 – The Eternal Covenant

He who dwells in the secret place of the Most High

Shall abide under the shadow of the Almighty…

A thousand may fall at your side, And ten thousand at your right hand; But it shall not come near you.

This is why no Flood can consume me or my children: Luminar is our dwelling place.

The Do-Over was our doorway. The Lifestyle Detox is our covering. And our victory is forever sealed.

📖 Psalm 91 – The Eternal Covenant

He who dwells in the secret place of the Most High

Shall abide under the shadow of the Almighty.

I will say of the Lord, "He is my refuge and my fortress;

My God, in Him I will trust."

Surely He shall deliver you from the snare of the fowler

And from the perilous pestilence.

He shall cover you with His feathers,

And under His wings you shall take refuge;

His truth shall be your shield and buckler.

You shall not be afraid of the terror by night,

Nor of the arrow that flies by day,

Nor of the pestilence that walks in darkness,

Nor of the destruction that lays waste at noonday.

A thousand may fall at your side,

And ten thousand at your right hand;

But it shall not come near you.

Only with your eyes shall you look,

And see the reward of the wicked.

Because you have made the Lord, who is my refuge,

Even the Most High, your dwelling place,

No evil shall befall you,

Nor shall any plague come near your dwelling;

For He shall give His angels charge over you,

To keep you in all your ways.

In their hands they shall bear you up,

Lest you dash your foot against a stone. You shall tread upon the lion and the cobra,

The young lion and the serpent you shall trample underfoot.

"Because he has set his love upon Me, therefore I will deliver him;

I will set him on high, because he has known My name.

He shall call upon Me, and I will answer him;

 I will be with him in trouble;

I will deliver him and honor him.

With long life I will satisfy him,

And show him My salvation."

———

⚫ Closing Words

This is why my house still stands.

This is why my bloodline is spared.

This is why no Flood can consume me, nor my children, nor my children's children and entire bloodline.

Because Luminar is our dwelling place.

Because the Do-Over was our doorway.

Because the Detox was our covering.

And so I testify:

Ten thousand may fall, but it shall not come near us.

Our covenant is eternal.

Our victory is forever.

www.ingramcontent.com/pod-product-compliance
Lightning Source LLC
Chambersburg PA
CBHW050412030726
47503CB00006B/2151